My Papa
saw the
Easter Bunny
in a cornfield in
Missouri

WRITTEN BY: ROBERT M. ETHIER

ILLUSTRATED BY: TONI R. D'ANGELO

AuthorHouse
1663 Liberty Drive
Bloomington, IN 47403
www.authorhouse.com
Phone: 1 (800) 839-8640

Published by AuthorHouse 07/26/2019

ISBN: 978-1-7283-2085-4 (sc)
ISBN: 978-1-7283-2086-1 (e)

Print information available on the last page.

Any people depicted in stock imagery provided by Getty Images are models,
and such images are being used for illustrative purposes only.
Certain stock imagery Getty Images.

This book is printed on acid-free paper.

Because of the dynamic nature of the Internet, any web addresses or links contained in this book may have changed
since publication and may no longer be valid. The views expressed in this work are solely those of the author and do not
necessarily reect the views of the publisher, and the publisher hereby disclaims any responsibility for them.

authorHOUSE®

This book is dedicated to Harbour, Calla, Chandler, Eric, Adrienne, Shannon, Michael, John, Sonya and Toni.

When my papa was a kid, he saw the Easter Bunny in a cornfield behind his house in Missouri. He was in his backyard when he saw smoke rising over the tops of the cornstalks way out in the field.

He told me, "I walked through the tall cornstalks for what seemed like forever, and finally I came to a big clearing."

He said, "In the middle of the clearing were three large pots on a campfire. In one of the pots there was chocolate melting, in another pot there were marshmallows melting, and in the third pot there was peanut butter. The whole area smelled like a candy store.

On the other side of the clearing, he saw gigantic piles of all kinds of candy. In one pile there were thousands of jelly beans of all different colors.

In the other pile there were thousands of chocolate Easter eggs. Some of them were wrapped in colored paper, and some seemed to be painted.

Then he saw a huge pile of a big chocolate Easter Bunnies. He said they were the biggest chocolate Easter Bunnies he had ever seen.

There were many piles of different types of Easter candy. There were even giant piles of Easter baskets, ready to be filled with candy and delivered.

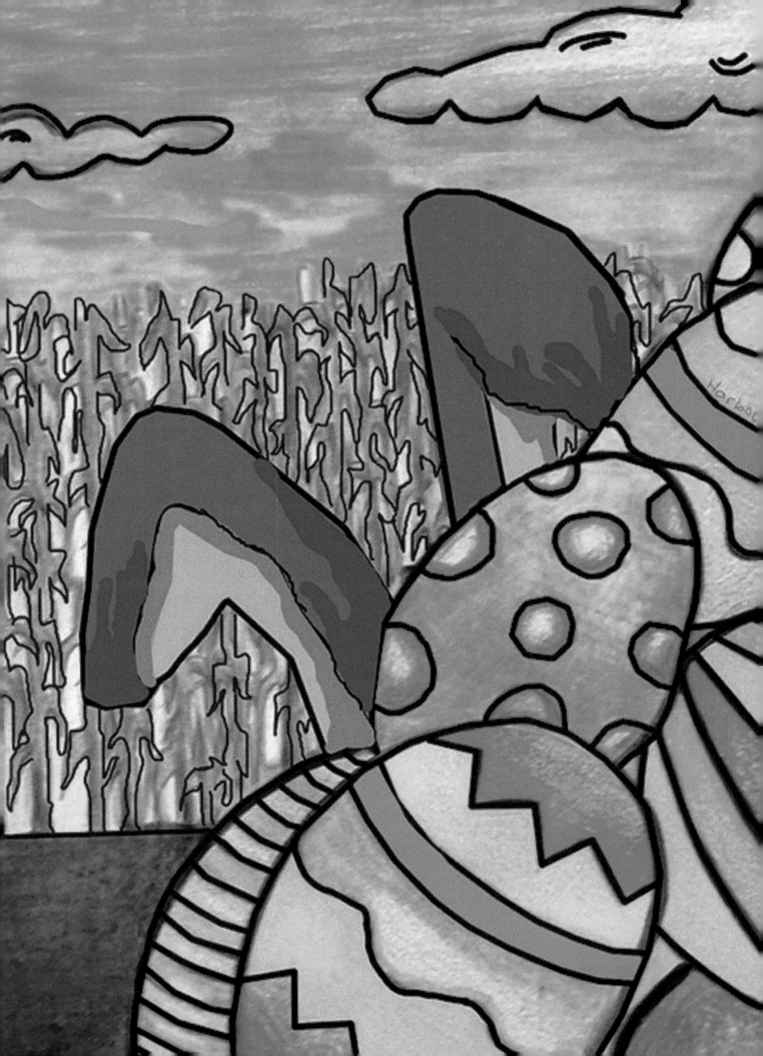

Then all of a sudden he heard a noise, and peeking around one of those piles was a great, big rabbit with very big ears. My papa was so scared that he wanted to run back home. Just then, the rabbit turned and looked right at him. Papa told me, "That's when I knew it was the Easter Bunny."

My papa said, "He looked at me, and his eyes were as big as a paper plates."

The Easter Bunny said, "Hey! Little boy! You should not be here! Nobody has ever seen me getting ready for Easter."

Papa said, "I'm sorry, Mr. Easter Bunny. I won't tell anybody where you are."

The Easter Bunny took my papa over to the giant pile of big chocolate bunnies and gave him one. He said, "Remember—do not tell anyone that you saw me. Now you had better go home because it will be dark soon."

As Papa was walking away, he turned around one last time to look at the Easter Bunny. He waved at him and said, "Goodbye, Easter Bunny. Don't worry, I'll keep it a secret."

Papa took his big chocolate bunny and started walking home through the cornfield.

When he got home, he put his chocolate Easter Bunny in his closet and ate a little piece of it every once in a while. He said, "It lasted a long time because it was a lot of chocolate for a little kid. I never saw the Easter Bunny ever again, but I didn't go looking for him either."

I think my papa was a very brave little kid, but no matter what, I am never ever going looking for the Easter Bunny.

CPSIA information can be obtained
at www.ICGtesting.com
Printed in the USA
BVHW022038040819
555064BV00021B/2403/P